Eleanor, Arthur, and Claire

Written and illustrated by Diana Engel

MACMILLAN PUBLISHING COMPANY   NEW YORK

MAXWELL MACMILLAN CANADA   TORONTO

MAXWELL MACMILLAN INTERNATIONAL

NEW YORK   OXFORD   SINGAPORE   SYDNEY

FOR AUNT MADY, UNCLE WALTER, AND AUNT CLAIRE...

AND FOR ELAINE.

Macmillan Publishing Company is part of the Maxwell Communication Group of Companies.
Macmillan Publishing Company 866 Third Avenue New York, NY 10022
Maxwell Macmillan Canada, Inc. 1200 Eglinton Avenue East
Suite 200 Don Mills, Ontario M3C 3N1
First edition
Printed in Hong Kong
1   3   5   7   9   10   8   6   4   2
The text of this book is set in 16 pt. Garamond.
The illustrations are rendered in ink and watercolor.
Library of Congress Cataloging-in-Publication Data
Engel, Diana.
Eleanor, Arthur, and Claire / written and illustrated by Diana Engel.
p.   cm.
Summary: Claire loves spending her summers with her grandparents,
and although she finds things changed after her grandfather's death
she and her grandmother find the strength to go on without him.
ISBN 0-02-733462-7
[1. Grandparents—Fiction. 2. Death—Fiction.] I. Title.
PZ7.E69874El 1992   [E]—dc20   90-21781

It was summer. Claire was staying with her Grandma and Grandpa in the country.

They always made a fuss when she arrived. "Oh Claire," said Grandma, "you've grown so tall!"

"And look," said Grandpa, "Claire has your hair color."

"The color my hair used to be," said Grandma.

Claire's grandparents, Eleanor and Arthur, were almost always busy.

Grandpa had a studio in the basement where he made clay sculptures of the most amazing design.

Grandma loved to paint and sketch. Her landscapes bloomed with color, and she was just beginning a handsome portrait of Arthur.

Side by side in the warm afternoons, they
worked happily, inside...

...and out.

One morning, after a particularly angry quarrel
the night before, Claire came downstairs. There on
the table were some very special gifts.

"What's all this?" she asked.

"Well," said Grandpa, "your Grandma and I get a
bit...stuck sometimes. Then I make her something
and she makes me something. Been doing it for
years."

Claire ate a big breakfast that morning.

"Let's go swimming!" she said.

"And pack a lunch!" said Grandma.

"And," said Grandpa, "let's not come home till dark."

"Oh," said Claire, as the days grew cooler, "I wish
it would never end."

"Don't worry," said Grandpa. "You'll be back
next summer."

Soon it was time for
Claire to return home.

She missed her grandparents and they missed
her...and life went on as usual.

Until the day Grandpa became sick. His heart
wasn't working well and he had to go to the hospital
in town.

Grandma visited every day. Claire sent letters
and beautiful drawings. But Grandpa grew weaker.

One day, in the middle of autumn, he died.

When all the ceremonies were over, Grandma
went to live with Claire's family, where she was
surrounded by those who loved her.
   But she kept her own house in the country.

A long, sad year passed, and it was summer again.

Grandma wanted to move back to her own home.

"Would you like to come, too?" she asked Claire.

Claire went, but she worried what the house
would feel like without her grandpa.

They had picnics and they had sing-alongs and
they played poker at night. But Claire could tell that
her grandma's heart just wasn't in it.
    She even found herself missing the old quarrels.

One morning, Claire came downstairs.

"Grandma," she said, "I've got an idea. I'll make
you something and you make me something. Then
we can surprise each other!"

Grandma's eyes opened wide. She stared at the
little girl with wonder.

"I'll try," she said.

Claire ran downstairs and began to work. She could imagine her grandpa standing next to her in the studio.

Upstairs, Grandma picked up her brushes and
looked for a canvas. There in the corner was the
unfinished portrait she had started last summer.
Could she finish it now?

She began. Slowly she brushed on the paint, layer by layer, while her memories of Arthur filled the room.

The two worked very hard, and soon the end of
the week arrived.

After supper, Claire and Grandma exchanged
their gifts.

The summer came to an end.
    Claire took home her painting and Grandpa's
clay and tools. She would have a lot to show
Grandma when she returned next year.

Grandma was already planning a large landscape.